BetwixtDream@gmail.com

Corinne, Corona, and Carissa couldn't wait to head to school. It had snowed last night and they ran straight for the yard and flung themselves into the snow.

Carissa began moving her arms and legs to make an angel in the snow. Corinne and Corona soon joined as they saw the beautiful angel on the ground that it formed. They laughed as they bounded across the yard to look at the artwork that they had made.

“We better get to school,” Corona said to her girlfriends.

Now, as fate would have it, a comet streaked 100 miles above, glowing brightly red. Its tail dazzled and looked like a rainbow: red, orange, yellow, green, blue, indigo and violet. It crossed overhead and flecks of its essence drifted down to the neighborhood below. Some of these flecks landed on the angels; still warm, it gently caressed the snow as it cooled.

Then, something magical began to happen: a wing began to flutter and a leg began to move. More motion appeared as bodies began to form. One angel stood up and stretched her wings. A second sat up and exercised her wings. The last angel floated over the ground as her wings lifted her up high.

Unbeknownst to the girls, their angels floated above them on their way to school overseeing their journey.

On their way to school, Corinne, Corona, and Carissa saw their friend Edmond by the Salvation Army and stopped to say hello.

“How are my friends doing today?” said Edmond.

THE SALVATION ARMY

“We’re going to school,” the girls replied.

“Edmond, how come you’re always outside this building every morning?” asked Corona.

“Well, my little angels, I stay here in this building because I lost my house to a fire,” Edmond said with sadness.

THE SALVATION ARMY

The girls didn't know what to say and felt so bad for their friend.

"Well, have a good day. Think good thoughts good things will happen," replied Edmond.

The girls continued on but couldn't stop talking about how they could help Edmond.

"I want to help Edmond find a home," beamed Carissa. "He's always been so nice and kind. Maybe we can try to find a place for Edmond."

After Mrs. Warfield finished her English lesson she turned to her class.

“I want everyone to know helping those who need help is as important as our History, Math and English lessons.”

"I want all of you to think how you can help someone during your holiday vacation. I want to teach you a poem that my mother taught me."

We call to the heavens and sky above
To rain down objects sending love
To those who struggle needing more
And make their lives better we implore.

Grade - 4
Sec - A
Class works
Subject- English
To Be
I am
You are
He/She/It is
We are
They are
Today's
Lessons
CLASS - 4
SEC - A

Corinne, Corona, and Carissa exchanged glances and smiles. They had a friend whom they knew they wanted to help.

MULTIPLICATION TABLE
YELLOW
YELLOW GREEN
YELLOW ORANGE
GREEN
ORANGE
BLUE GREEN
RED ORANGE
BLUE
RED
BLUE VIOLET
RED VIOLET
VIOLET

As the bell rang, the girls couldn't wait to run outside and begin their holiday vacation. The school day was finally over and they wanted to help Edmond.

Carissa said to Corinne and Corona, “Let’s hold hands and say Mrs. Warfield’s poem. We can think about Edmond and hope it helps him.”

We call to the heavens and sky above
To rain down objects sending love
To those who struggle needing more
And make their lives better we implore.

The girlfriends headed towards home and smiled as they approached Edmond.

“Why, hello Carissa, Corona and Corrine. I've got good news. My brother bought a house and he's going to let me live with him. I'm so happy and know that your love helped me. Think good thoughts and good things will happen. I won't see you every day in front of the Salvation Army but I will think about all of you each day.”

1758

"This is the best gift ever, Edwin!" shouted Corrine.

As the children approach their yards, anticipation rose as they looked for their snow angels. Their eyes opened wide as they saw that their snow angels weren't there.

"Our angels are gone," shouted Corona.

Made in the USA
Middletown, DE
01 December 2025

23225086R00020